LOVE TO LAST A LIFETIME

SUSAN MEACHEN

CONTENTS

Author Moto	5
Chapter 1	7
Chapter 2	9
Chapter 3	13
Chapter 4	19
Chapter 5	27
Chapter 6	31
Chapter 7	35
Chapter 8	41
Chapter 9	45
Chapter 10	51
Epilogue	57
Acknowledgments	59

E-BOOK ISBN: B08LMZP7SZ
ISBN: 9798551801993

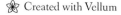 Created with Vellum

AUTHOR MOTO

Be Unique Be You Be Beautiful
~Author Susan Meachen

CHAPTER ONE

September 1958

From the moment I laid eyes on Greta, I knew she was meant to be loved by me for a lifetime. She'd been talking to my best friend's girlfriend and her smile drew me in like a moth to a flame. Who would have ever guessed our story would be one for the ages?

We were from two different worlds my family was filthy rich and Greta's family was dirt poor. It didn't bother me any. Chasing her that Autumn became my favorite hobby. The more I chased her the more she ran but nothing was going to change my mind she would be mine.

My family may have been filthy rich but my father had the mindset everyone worked for what they got. So, I worked long hours at the family business and made a paycheck just like everyone else. Everything I had was earned and it made me proud to know at twenty-five I owned everything and had money to spare or blow anyway I deemed worthy and Greta was so worthy.

Every time my best friend Jason went out with Karen, I

bugged him to let me follow along. Greta was new to our town she didn't seem to have many friends other than Karen so they spent a lot of time together. After about four of their dates that I crashed, Karen finally spoke up. "Ethen just ask her out so Jason and I can have one date without you showing up."

"That sounds simple enough Karen but if you haven't noticed she doesn't seem to like me even a little."

"Because you're a rich snob most of the time come down to her level. You can do it your best friends with Jason and he's far from rich."

That night on my way back home I thought about what Karen had said. It was true all of my friends were working-class people I felt comfortable around them. None of us tried to compete with the other we all just enjoyed hanging out together. With that finally settled as I walked into my place, I drop my keys on the table and hung my jacket up. Tomorrow will be the start of our lives together even if she doesn't know it.

CHAPTER TWO

Dreaming of Hope

G oing to lunch the following day I make my way down to the small café that's around the corner from my family's business. This is going to be my normal lunch place 'til Greta gives in and goes out with me. Found out from Jason last night she had started working there last week. Walking into the café a young chipper blonde bounces up to me.

"You want a table sir or the counter?" Looking over her head I search the place for Greta spotting her working the counter. "Counter is fine thank you." Walking around her making my way to the last barstool sitting down I pull a menu from the stack on the counter. Looking it over they have a special of the day but a burger and fries look good.

"Sorry for your wait what can I get you to drink?" She hasn't even looked at me yet she's just holding her little pad in her hand.

"Sweet tea would be great; sweetheart and I'll take a burger and fries also." when she hears my voice her head jerks up and she glares at me then hisses at me "why are you here?"

"uh, food it's what everyone is here for I assume. Now if you'd like to discuss where we should have our first date that is also a good reason to be here."

"Why can't you just take a hint? I don't date out of my league us as anything more than friends isn't ever happening Ethan, your order will be up shortly."

The older man beside me laughs out loud "She seems to have a temper with you, son. That one is always happy but you made her do a three-sixty in mere seconds. What did you do?"

"Asked her out."

This routine is done for two weeks before she finally looks at me and asks the simplest question. "What does it take to make you go away?"

"That's simple sweetheart go out with me one time is all it'll take."

"Why is that all it will take what does that even mean?"

"Simply you'll enjoy yourself and we will go out again afterward."

As she fills my glass back-up, she looks me in the eye. "Fine one date that's all I can promise but I get to pick the place."

"Sounds good let me know where we are going here is my number to my office and my home. You figure out what you want to do and we can make plans. Call me sweetheart." As I'm dropping money on the counter for my lunch and her tip. Walking back into the office I actually feel happy for the first time in almost a month. Now just got to make sure whatever she decides we enjoy doing together.

Finishing my day at the office I stop at my sectaries desk to see if I had any messages before I make my way to the elevator. How long will the woman make me dangle in the wind before she puts me out of my misery of not knowing? Tonight, is dinner with my parents. Guilt makes me do it a couple of nights a week. They only had one child no one ever speaks of, why there were no siblings I'm not sure, but it couldn't have been by my mother's choice. If it was possible, she'd still have me living at home with a curfew. There's no time to run home and change running late leaving the office has me barely arriving for dinner. Mother is very strict with rules of etiquette and manners no elbows on the table men must stand till the ladies have been seated. It's annoying but it made me into a gentleman at least. Dinner is going great before my father speaks up.

"Ethan, you ever get that young lady from the café to go out with you?"

That queued my mother to ask questions. "You're seeing someone, Ethan? Why am I just hearing of this? Does she come from a good family?"

"First no I'm not seeing anyone just yet she's thinking on it which means there was nothing to tell you and third I know very little about her family they are new to the area."

"Ethan honey it's important to remember you need to marry someone who is of our status. Anyone outside of our status in life will forever feel out of place. Also, Ethan, your children will inherit all your grandfather and father worked so hard to build. It's best to remember that."

"Mother don't worry about something that is years away still."

Dinner with the parents was eventful, to say the least. Unlocking the door at home I can hear the phone ringing in my office rushing in I grab it on the final ring "Hello"

"Are you busy Ethan you seem to be out of breath?"

"No just getting in from having dinner with my

parents. Did you decided what we are going to do on this date you agreed to?"

"Yes, it's all I've thought of since you left the café today. Ethan, I have to give it to you, you're the first man to ever chase me this hard. What if we just go to the county fair Saturday night?"

"Greta you amaze me at times, we could go anywhere there is no limit and you want to go to the county fair? If that is your wish then that is what we will do."

"It's the easiest thing to do and we both will know others there so it won't be that awkward first date. Goodnight Ethan hope you have a nice day at work tomorrow."

She doesn't even wait for me to respond the line just goes silent before it makes that awful screeching sound when the phone has been off the hook too long. Goodnight beautiful.

The rest of the week seems to drag by even though every day I'm at the café fighting to get a seat at the counter for lunch. On Friday when I step into the café there is a little sign in front of the last barstool.

Reserved for the most persistent man on earth 🤍

Taking the seat, the guy beside me whispers "that little brunette will kick you out of that spot sir. She has run off three other guys already it must be reserved for her boyfriend or something."

"I'll take my chances just to see her is worth it in the end."

"That's the truth this lunch counter hasn't ever been the most wanted seat in this place. Now guys wait just to sit here. Good luck"

Laughing a little to myself I think no luck needed this seat was saved for me.

CHAPTER THREE

October

Saturday evening to be taking forever to get here for the first time in my life I wish I didn't have a housekeeper. There is nothing to do at my house other than work for the company and it's not happening today as it can sometimes turn my moods sour. About one in the afternoon I put on my running shoes and head for the outskirts of town for a run on the trails in the hills. Running it's one of the very few things I do just for me it's a stress release it gives me a rush unlike anything else ever has. Stopping at the top of the fourth hill I glance at my watch it's almost four, time to turn back and head for home. The date I've worked so hard to get is almost here.

When I cross into the other side of town some people in the neighborhood stare at me as I pass by. It's not a new thing to have people look at me I drive a car that costs more money than their homes do. Pulling up in front of the house Greta had given me the address to it is a reminder of how different our worlds are. The little yellow house has chipping paint coming off the outside the walkway to the front door has weeds growing up between the cracks. Stepping up onto the more dirt than board porch I knock on the door. When the door has opened a crack, a little blonde-headed girl looks up at me "you here for my sister mister?"

"Is your sister Greta?"

"Yes, she is."

"Then yes I'm here for your sister."

"Gracie, what have we told you about opening the door to strangers?"

She scolds the little girl as she pulls the door open. "Sorry she's not supposed to answer the door but she's a little brat and does it anyway."

Holding the car door open for her she smiles at me "You are a true southern gentleman, aren't you?"

"It has been drilled into me since I was old enough to walk so guess I am."

The ride out to the county fairgrounds is a bit awkward the silence seems to stretch on forever but the drive isn't but about twenty minutes. Once we are out of the car, she lets me take her hand as we walk through the gates. We walk the outside edge of the fairground just looking around looking to see if any of our friends have shown up.

"Want something to snack on Greta or maybe just a drink?"

"A cherry soda would be good."

"Want a snack or anything?"

She just shakes her head at me as I order her soda handing it to her, I follow her line of sight and see the games set up across from the snack stand.

I tug her hand as we make our way over to the ring toss. "Want to play?"

"No sports were never my strong point in school I'll pass."

"Then pick a prize that you like and point it out."

"No, Ethan these games aren't fair they take people's money. It's just a waste."

Motioning the guy who has been screaming at all the young couples that are passing by.

"Give me ten rings we want that big bear."

"Good luck boy you need to land all of those rings to win that bear."

In a matter of minutes, Greta is holding that bear and the guy is screaming "you cheated somehow that hasn't ever happened."

Jason and Karen walk over to us "Nice bear Greta where did you find it?"

"Ethan won it over at that game."

"Look Jason people win the games you just can't play is all."

Jason is like a brother to me but his company isn't wanted tonight but it seems Greta and Karen had different plans for us all. We've all rode every ride in the park and the Ferris wheel twice it's starting to get cool and dark. As much as I hate the idea it's time to take Greta home. Leaving the fairgrounds, we all head to our cars and Greta takes my hand this time.

"I had a really great time Ethan it's been a long time since I had that much fun. Seems like all I do now that school is done is work and go home. Doesn't leave a lot of time for fun anymore."

"We'll need to fix that in the future. Greta's life is meant to be enjoyed only working robs you of life's greatest thing which is having fun. Hopefully, tonight leads to another date.?"

Pulling up outside her house she looks towards the house then back at me. "You actually want to go out again?"

"Wouldn't be here at all if I didn't intend for this to go somewhere. Unlike a lot of guys dating isn't a sport for me."

She leans over and kisses my cheek "then you plan the next one and let me know when it is. I've got to go inside my parents will be waiting up on me. Bye, Ethan."

From that night on we are together every spare minute we have. She's not taken me home to meet her parents but neither have I. Don't get me wrong my parents are great parents but they have a certain standard for me to meet when it comes to dating or liking a girl enough to bring home. Figure if we keep seeing each other in a couple a week's I'll take her home to meet my parents.

Greta works on average six days a week but she never runs out of energy it seems. The girl has a smile on her face all the time but don't let that fool you. Her temper is hot and she doesn't back down from any challenge. Standing beside my car in the café's parking lot I argue with her about going to my parents this weekend for dinner.

"Greta it won't be bad the food will be good and I got to prove to my mom you're real. She will love you my dad knows who you are and he has never said anything bad about you. Sweetheart here lately I've ditched my dinners with them to be with you. One dinner is all I ask."

"Fine but you have to agree to come to dinner at my parents' house. They ask questions about you all the time and honestly, the answers they won't I don't have."

"Deal what questions you need answers to sweetheart?"

"Nothing my parents think you are going to break my heart. We are from two different worlds Ethan you already know this. No one sees us staying together which means one or both of us are going to get hurt in the end."

"Sweetheart I'm not going to break your heart it's something that I'd love to have forever. Do you plan to break mine?"

"No, never! But I do have dreams Ethan going on to college is something I'm willing to work for every day if need be."

Pulling her close I kiss her cheek and give her a tight hug. "You want a ride home it's getting cold?"

CHAPTER FOUR

November

September and October seemed to speed right on by in a blink of an eye. It's the first of November and somehow, I talked Greta into coming to dinner with me tonight at my parents. It certainly is better than bringing her home for the first time on a holiday. Pulling through the gates at my parents' home Greta takes a deep breath that I can hear over the radio that is playing. Smiling over at her she is a bit paler than she was when I picked her up.

"You good sweetheart?"

"Ethan, I knew your parents had money but how much money do they really have? They are both going to look at me and see me as a gold digger. This is a bad idea let's not go in."

"What no they won't think that. They are going to love you as much as I do."

With that slip, we both turn and look at each other. "Did you mean that Ethan?"

"I said it so yes, it is true."

"Oh, thank God! I've been biting my tongue for weeks now. I think I fell in love with you the first night. What do we do now?"

"Go in my parents' house would be a good start they are staring at us... But this conversation isn't over just yet."

She looks out her window then smiles "deal we will finish this later."

The way she said that has me adjusting my slacks as I go around the back of the car. That look said so much and so did her comment now we have to sit through dinner with my parents sitting across from each other. As we all settle in the dining room the staff brings in the first course. Looking across at Greta her nose is a little crinkled as she looks at the soup. When I catch her eye, I wink at her and nod my head at the soup. "It's amazing, I promise. It's one of Nelle's specialties. Try it."

With my urging, she takes a small spoonful of the roasted carrot soup that Nelle has been making for me all my life. Watching her closely as she puts the spoon into her mouth I watch as her eyes close as the delicious flavor explodes in her mouth. That was almost as enjoyable as sex but not quite. She holds her own with my mom when she quizzes her about her job.

"Working as a waitress doesn't pay a lot but it's helping me save to go to college next year."

"Yes, mother, she is planning to pay her way through school that speaks volumes about her work ethic."

"Ethan I was just being polite. Greta, dear it's wonderful you have dreams and hopefully, they will all come true."

After that conversation, I think we've had enough time with my parents my father will have a talk with mother after we leave. Once again, she valued someone on what they make at a job and not the person. Holding the door open for Greta she giggles a little. "She doesn't like me Ethan told you they would think I was a gold digger."

"No, my mother is just a snob my father likes you and will talk to her before we make it out the gate."

Once we are back on the road headed to her side of town, she touches my hand, "Do we have to end the night right now? There's a conversation that started earlier that I, personally would like to finish."

Sitting at the red-light in town that separates the two parts of the city. We just look at each other both of us asking the same question with just our eyes.

"Where would you like to go, Greta, we can go to the café, lovers overlook, or my place? Two of them give us privacy but the choice is yours to make."

Watching as she chews the corner of her lip, she looks right then left then she licks her lips for moisture before speaking "Your place sounds like the best place."

"My house it is then. It's about ten minutes from here."

Neither of us speak a word for the next ten minutes or so then we pull into my driveway.

"You have a nice house, Ethan. Is it a rental or do you own it? Oh, that sounds so bad out loud."

"It doesn't come on and I own my home it was the first thing I bought. It was my escape from my parents' house so it was a goal I set for myself."

Unlocking the front door, I hold the door open for her, and the heat from inside washes over us both. As she passes by the faint smell of vanilla still clings to her it was one of the first things, I noticed about her when we met. Turning the lights on in the family room she takes a seat on the sofa in the far corner as she can get.

"Greta are you scared of being here? Sweetheart please

know I'll never ask you to do anything you're not ready to do we have a lifetime in front of us."

"I'm not scared of you Ethan this is just something I've never done before and I'm a little nervous is all. How do we do this is there a certain way this happens?"

"We talk it's the whole reason we came here. Would you like a drink or a snack maybe have no clue what's in the kitchen but we can look? What I do know is there is cherry soda in there."

Walking into the kitchen she's right on my heels. "Why do you have cherry soda in your refrigerator you told me it was nasty at the fair on our first date?"

"Because I knew this day was going to come and I wanted to have stuff here that you like. When you're here I want you to feel comfortable and at home."

"As a first boyfriend, you are setting the bar really high for any future men in my life. Not that I have any want for another one just saying sorry I get all chatty when I'm nervous and say stuff I shouldn't say."

"Sweetheart, slow down. Breathe, it's okay."

She sits down at the table in the kitchen she smiles at me when I sit her drink in front of her. Everything about her is perfect from her small perk nose to her dark doe eyes. Reaching over I brush the hair from her cheek so we can make eye contact.

"What would you like to talk about? We both have done admitted we are in love with the other. Guess that leaves us at a great starting point. Greta, I've never told another woman that I loved them. We both are in a position that neither of us has been in before. From my point of view, we do what is best for us and our relationship."

Watching as she takes a sip of her soda waiting for her response is nerve-wracking.

"If that is the way you see it then we are on the same page and we can move forward in our relationship. Whatever that may be."

Leaning across the table I seal our lips together lightly tracing her lips with my tongue has her opening her mouth and letting me in to taste her. When she cuts the kiss off short, I'm shocked when she gets out of her chair and climbs on my lap. As she drapes her arms around my neck there is no hiding how turned on, I am instead of pulling away she tightens her hold on me before she starts to kiss me. Wrapping my arm around her waist I pull her closer as our tongues intertwine like lovers. Breaking the kiss, I whisper against her lips "we need to stop sweetheart or we are going end up in my room" I can feel the smile she just gave me "and that would be a bad thing?"

Pulling back from her I study her face for any form of regret or shame. Locking eyes with her "you know once we ring the bell it can't be unrung? There's no doubt in my heart you're the person that I want to spend the rest of my life with but you need to be certain of that also."

"Ethan you are my one true love if I had any doubt about it then we wouldn't be here right now." She leans in close to my ear and whispers "make love to me Ethan"

That's all the encouragement needed pushing further back from the table I scoop her ass up in my hands and head towards my bedroom. Sitting her down on the edge of the bed I watch her face for any worry or fear none even registers. Then she stands up and starts to unbutton the front of her dress. Following her lead, I undo my shirt and toss it to the floor. We silently stare at each other as she undoes more buttons and I do my belt and slacks. I'm about to have a stroke when she pushes her dress off her shoulders and it flutters to the floor around her feet leaving her in her underclothes. Tonight, is going to be the best night of my life. As she unfastens her bra and pushes it off her shoulders, I push my boxers off. Watching as she does a quick glance down my body I watch as the blush spreads across her face. Reaching out I touch her shoulder "sweetheart are you sure this is what you want to do? We can stop right now if it's what you would like to do."

"No, Ethan I want you to make love to me. Neither of us has doubts where this is going to lead us. We love each other and one day we will be married so I want you to be my first and last lover."

Watching as she pushes her underwear down off her hips, I suck a breath between my teeth that lets out a low whistle. When she climbs on my bed my brain turns to mush and I follow her onto the bed. Leaning over her I balance myself on one hand as my other smooths her hair as our lips connect. For the last few months, this is all I could think about was having Greta in my bed committing herself to me and only me forever. Tracing the line of her face down to her neck my fingers ghost across her skin as I make my way down to her left breast palming it in my hand her skin is so smooth her nipple is pebble hard and a dusty rose color. Sucking the nipple into my mouth she arches off the bed as she locks her hands around my head pulling me closer to her breast. Pulling her hands from the back of my head I kiss each one before laying them down beside her. Then I do light nip's down her body as I make my way down to pussy pushing her legs apart. She blushes the prettiest shade of red as I settle between her thighs sliding my arms under her thighs, I grip her hips in my hands as the first taste of her pussy touches my tongue. With the first touch of my tongue, Greta tries to set-up but I hold her hips down urging her to lay back down. "Sweetheart just relax and enjoy the pleasure"

As she settles back onto the mattress, I pick up the pace as I devour her pussy and she tugs my hair trying to bring us closer together. It's rewarding to know I'll be the only man who will ever get to see her come undone when she reaches her release. Lifting my mouth from her I press my thumb against her clit and apply just a little pressure and watch as she tosses her head from side to before she screams my name into the void of my bedroom. Watching her float back down from her release is just as beautiful as watching her have her first orgasm from my mouth and hands. Climbing back up over her I kiss her deeply letting her taste herself from my tongue.

"Ethan that was the most amazing thing I've ever felt in my life. Did you enjoy it also? Please tell me if I am doing something wrong. No one ever told me that the woman enjoyed sex it was just implied we were to do it for our husbands. How can other women not enjoy that? It was the best thing in the whole world. What do we do next?"

Slipping to the side of her I smile down at her, "glad you enjoyed it sweetheart making love should always be enjoyed by both not just the man. As for what is next, I'd suggest you breathe before you pass out. We can stop right now if you'd like."

As she pushes my shoulder, she smirks at me "uh there is no way we are stopping now we just got started. What do we do next? Should I kiss your body? Don't know how all of that will fit in my mouth but I'll try if you want me to. Lord, I'm rambling, aren't I? Sure, you don't want to take me home now?"

Bringing her face close to mine I kiss her lips with quick

pecks till she stops trying to talk. "Sweetheart you can do whatever you want to do there is no rule to lovemaking."

"Ethan, I've never done this before what if I mess up?"

Easing myself back over her I lean down to kiss her again to make her stop talking. Settling between her thighs lining the head of my cock at her entrance I painfully ask one more time "are you sure about this Greta?" Her response is to tilt her hips towards me letting my dick slide in just a little. Bracing myself on my forearms I hold perfectly still. "Sweetheart, open your eyes and look at me. This will hurt for just a few seconds before the pain disappears, do you understand?" she nods her head yes as I push further into her warmth then I feel the thin barrier before pushing my way through it. Watching her face, a couple of tears drip from the corners of her eyes where she has them squeezed shut. Stalling I let her grow accustomed to the feeling of having me inside her body before I start to move slowly in and out of her drenched pussy her juices are making it easy to be gentle with her. Slowly she opens her eyes and she watches me as my thrust becomes quicker and deeper. With my own release within reach, I watch as her eyelids flutter and her breathing becomes shallow pausing for a moment the thought of no birth control pops into my thought but it quickly disappears as her inner muscles clench my dick milking it for every drop of come I have in me. As a chill runs down my spine, I pull her close to my chest and whisper her name into her hair "Greta, I love you."

CHAPTER FIVE

December

Since that night in November when we first made love every free moment, we get to be together had us at my house naked in about every room in the house. Greta is so open and free being her first made it easier to get her to try new things and in new places. There's not one room in my house we haven't fucked in that includes the garage now. She was laid across the hood of my car when I turned from closing the garage door then she'd told me to fuck her. With her ass in the air, I rip her underwear trying to jerk them to the side so I could shove my hard cock into her tight folds. Every time we fuck, she is drenched. Slowing the pace, I pull my cock out and slide it up and down the crack of her ass pushing a little every time I come in contact with her asshole. "Sweetheart one day soon I'm going to fuck you in the ass and you're going to enjoy it so much the orgasm will steal your breath away. Does that sound like something you'd like to try?"

Listening to the small little gasp she is letting out lets

me know she's not going to be talking as it is almost impossible for her to do. As she tosses her hair across her shoulder the look in her eyes when she turns her head towards me is the look, she's given me every time we try something new. Slipping back into her warmth I give her and myself what we both want. Standing behind her with my dick still in her we both catch our breath as I rub her back and feel my cum start to drip down her legs. Come on sweetheart let's get us cleaned up before we got to be at your parents for dinner. One thing for certain is she was a shy virgin when we started dating but she is a freak behind closed doors now. One day soon when it's not so cold out I will talk her into making love in public. There's a bit of satisfaction in knowing I was the one who taught her everything she knows about sex. Being her first and her last is an honor nothing or anyone can take away from me.

When we arrive outside her parents' house, she turns to me "Ethan we can leave anytime you're ready there's no rule that says we have to stay for the whole evening."

"Don't worry sweetheart you made it through my parents' dinner I'm sure I can survive a dinner with your family."

"I'll remind you of that later when we do escape. Also, don't forget Gracie will be at the table so that means talking with her mouth full of food."

"Greta don't stress over this too much. we have to learn to be around each other's family if we plan to get married one day. That is still what we plan to do right?"

"Of course, we are still planning to get married unless you're having second thoughts."

Opening her door, I give her a hand out of the car. "No, I've not changed my mind never will. You are stuck with me for life sweetheart."

Meeting Greta's parents is an adventure within itself Ricky is a contract which he explains is a day laborer and Connie is a full-time wife and mother. Then there is the lovely little Gracie that Greta loves so much she's like a mini-tornado tearing through the house. Their home is simple nothing big and showy like my family my mom demands the best of everything and Connie seems content to just have her family. Dinner is a simple meal of meatloaf, green beans, mashed potatoes, and some kind of cobber for dessert. Ricky quizzes me on my job how I enjoy working for the family business. All the things a good father should do when a young man is courting his daughter. When the table goes silent Gracie looks up then she smiles

"You going to marry my sister Ethan? If so, can I be in the wedding? I promise to even wear a dress the whole day."

"We've not decided on that just yet Gracie but I bet your sister will let you know if we decide to."

Sitting in the small living room we watch a Christmas special on the small television before I leave for the evening. Greta walks me out to the car standing on the sidewalk she gives me a quick peck on the lips.

"Hope my parents didn't scare you off they are a bit much at first but you did good with them and thank you for being so nice to Gracie."

"They were very nice sweetheart don't worry about it all parents embarrass their children... But your parents were calm compared to mine. Goodnight sweetheart." Leaning in close I give her a quick kiss before pulling away as the front light flicks on and off.

It's a week before Christmas nothing I've looked at yet screams Greta to me she deserves special gifts with lots of meaning behind the gift. Standing in the small jewelry store a couple of blocks from my office I look at necklaces, bracelets, even a couple of rings. Nothing is calling out to me. This would be so much easier if she would just give me a hint of something, she would like but she refuses since I wouldn't give her any ideas on what I'd like. Heading towards the exit I spot something out of the corner of my eye it's a beautiful ring with a Sapphire stone set in the middle of diamonds. Getting the sales clerk to come over I hold the ring inspect it, it's perfect giving it back to the clerk I tell her to box it up. There's no denying it the thought of asking Greta to marry me has been in my mind for months now. Seems it's time to talk to her father and see if he will give me permission to marry his daughter.

Monday afternoon I stop by the garage Ricky works at

"Afternoon sir wanted to see if you'd like to go to lunch. Want to talk to you about something."

"Figured you be by sooner than later. Guess you want to ask permission to marry my daughter. Ethan, son, she's not from your world she'll never be from your world. She has dreams big dreams you could help her fulfill her dreams. Will you be able to protect her in your world? Your life will not be disrupted but Greta's whole world will be flipped upside down if she marries you. Promise never to hurt my little girl and you have my blessing. Now that's all done where do you plan to take your future father-in-law for lunch?"

"Didn't think that far ahead sir what would you like, sir?"

Christmas comes and passes we spend time with both sets of parents.

CHAPTER SIX

New Year's Eve

Tonight, is the night the perfect date has been planned. We are going to the New Year's party at my parent's country club. Going to ask Greta at the stroke of midnight to be my wife. Even the best-laid plans can be derailed in a matter of seconds no minutes are needed. The New Year's party was going great till an old girlfriend arrived and rumors ran amuck and derailed my proposal to Greta. What's one more night

Two weeks have passed since the party and I'm sitting in my office looking out over the city. It's a cold blustery January day nothing about it makes it a memorable day same as any other day. Then my secretary buzzes my intercom "Mr. Carter you have a visitor at the front desk. What would you like for us to do?"

"Marlene, do you know who is at the front desk? That would make it easier to tell you what to do."

"Sorry, sir it's a young lady Greta Sample."

"Show her to my office I'll see her."

When Marlene leads Greta into my office I rise from my seat at my desk and motion towards the seating area. "Hello, sweetheart. What brings you by today?"

"Wanted to see you is all and maybe talk you into lunch."

"Thank you, Marlene." I motion for her to leave the office. "Now Ms. Sample what has you sitting in my office this afternoon? We've been dating for months and not once have you popped up at my office."

Watching Greta fidget under my watchful eye has me on high alert something is off.

"Ethan, we love each other, right? Nothing will or would ever change that right?"

"Of course, we love each other nothing will ever change that sweetheart. Tell me what is wrong whatever it is we will deal with it together."

"Oh, this is hard to explain. Ethan my aunt didn't come last month she always comes on time. I need to see a doctor I know this but if my parents find out they will disown me. What are we going to do? This isn't something that can be hidden for a long period of time, this will be obvious in a couple more months. The one thing I swore would never happen to me has happened to me. I know it took both of us to do this but it's my life it will destroy along with my future."

Watching Greta as she runs her hands down her skirt. "Sweetheart, are you trying to tell me we are having a baby?" Dear Lord this isn't the way I ever envisioned my life unfolding I planned to purpose to Greta then she and our moms could plan the perfect wedding. In a few years, we would discuss and plan for a family. Taking a couple of deep breaths, I retrieve my jacket from the hook on the door patting it down I pull the ring box from my pocket. Walking back to the sitting area I sit beside Greta and pull her hand into mine. "Sweetheart I wanted to make this so special for us both but it has been my intent for over a month now to ask you to marry me. Will you please do me the greatest honor in the world and become my wife and the mother of our future children?"

"Ethan, I didn't come down here expecting a marriage proposal."

"Well you're here now the question is asked please don't leave me hanging in the balance."

"Ethan I would love to be your wife and the future mother of our children." Watching as she lightly touches her stomach my heart flutters.

"Come on let's go eat lunch we'll need to speed the marriage along a little so people don't gossip so much about the timing not matching up."

We eat in a quiet secluded little restaurant and discuss how we will approach our parents with the need to speed the marriage forward quickly.

"Ethan your mom is going to forever hate me now. Everyone from this point forward will think I trapped you into marrying me. Oh Lord, they are going to gossip about us behind closed doors. Our children will hear these things in the future this will forever cast a shadow across our lives."

"Greta stop sweetheart take a deep breath. Once we are married for a few years this will fade to nothing no one will remember how long we were married before our first child was born. As long as we remember the reason, we got married who cares what others think."

CHAPTER SEVEN

Binding Ties and Family Times

Seems like it's been months since Greta told me we were going to have a baby. My dad was supportive of my choice to marry Greta my mother on the other hand was not thrilled with the idea until she learned she was going to be a grandmother. Greta begged that we keep the baby a secret from her parents till after the wedding. Our wedding date is less than a month away from her and my mom has dragged poor Greta all over the city looking at patterns for everything. At first, she held onto her job at the diner but after a couple of weeks of nausea non-stop and shopping trips that took hours to do. We agreed it was best if she went ahead and turned in her notice. There has been a couple of family dinners which include both of our parents it was tense at first but it's gotten easier. Mr. Sample made it clear he could not afford a Country Club wedding and I assured him it wasn't a problem. This is mine and Greta's wedding I have no issue with paying for what my future wife wants.

Sitting in my office I'm waiting for my afternoon meeting with my personal attorney. My whole world changed the night Greta told me we were going to be parents. Everything is about Greta and the baby now if something happens to either one of us, I want to make sure the other is financially secure to care for our baby.

"Afternoon Mr. Carter hear congratulations are in order. She's a beauty Ethan you are a very lucky young man. What are we doing today?"

"I need all my assets to be shared with Greta if something happens to me, she needs to be taken care of. My parents have been my beneficiaries all my adult life but that needs to be changed."

"You sure you want to do that so quickly in your relationship or what will be your marriage? Do you truly know this young lady enough to sign your life's work to her? This marriage is a little rushed is there more to this that as your attorney I need to know about?"

"There's nothing to tell Malcolm she will become my wife in a week and that means I need to take care of her and our future family."

Once the meeting is over and all the forms are signed it gives me a little peace of mind. From the moment Greta told me that we were going to have a baby my view of the world changed.

Pulling up outside Greta's parents' house I sit in the car for a few minutes watching the activity in the front window. Gracie is standing on something as she is in the thick of whatever is happening in the room. Getting out of the car the biting cold of January has me moving up the walkway a little faster than normal. Knocking on the door Gracie opens it just a crack "you're not allowed in the house anymore! Greta has on her pretty dress and they said you can't come in."

Squatting down in front of her "hi Gracie girl can you tell your sister I'm here we have plans this evening?"

"I'll tell her but you still can't come in," as she screams at Greta, she closes the door in my face.

The wait on the porch is fairly quick but long enough to have me shivering from the cold when Mrs. Sample opened the front door. "Sorry, Ethan we were doing the final fitting of the gown. She's convinced she has gained weight but it fit just like it did the day she picked it out. Coming on in she is getting ready. Are you getting nervous yet only a week away and your bachelor days will be over?"

"Not nervous at all the next week can't get here fast enough."

"I think both of you are a little excited."

Watching as Greta walks into the room it's like life slows down, I can see her hair sway, the smile that lights her face up when she sees me the way her lashes briefly touch her face when she blinks. When she stops in front of me, she leans up and kisses my cheek.

"Hi, sweetheart you ready to go pick out our wedding bands?"

"Been looking forward to it all day let's go."

———

Wedding Day
February 16, 1959

OUR WEDDING DAY arrives with a small snow covering the world outside and temperatures well below freezing. Greta picked this date said it was a lucky day that meant we'd forever be connected. Since she had picked the date, I picked the time of our wedding it will start at sunset. We'd both agreed there were to be no bachelor or bachelorette parties.

About an hour ago Jason showed up to keep me company, he's also riding with me to the church that way he can bring my car home. Greta and I will leave the reception in one of my family cars which will drive us to the airport. Then we are boarding a jet for Hawaii for two weeks of sun, sand, sex, and time to get used to being married. Arriving at the church we go to the groom's room to get changed and to make sure everyone has everything. Patting my pockets there's no bulge of a ring box. As my panic starts to rise Jason nudges my shoulder

"Calm down man I got the rings they are safe in my pocket. Quit worrying so much this is supposed to be the happiest day of your life but you've been off all day. Man, are you having cold feet? If you are be a man and walk away now."

Shoving him back with some force I look him in the eye "I have no second thought no cold feet this is what I've been waiting for all my life. Greta is my whole world she finally gives my life meaning."

"I know she is Ethan all of us knew from the first night you saw her last year. I've been your best friend since kindergarten."

Nodding my head at him I scrub my hands down my face "how much longer do we have to wait?"

"Time to go Ethan just got to get you to the alter in time for you to see Greta come down the aisle."

Walking down the aisle with my best friend and three of our closest friends makes me smile. We all have been friends since our childhood days. I was the odd one out between our group of five but not once did they make me feel different. My father was determined and demanded I go to school like any other child no boarding schools. His determination made me into the man I am today it also cemented my friendships for life. Standing at the altar with my best friend standing on one side of me and the priest standing on the other side. I keep my eyes glued to the back of the church as all the bridesmaids walk down the aisle and take their place, then the doors open up to Karen who is the maid of honor she's Greta's best friend. A quick thought comes to mind does she know Greta is pregnant, shaking my head to clear all thoughts of anything else from my mind. Then the wedding march starts and everyone stands as the double doors open to my beautiful Greta standing at the end of the aisle in her white lace gown it makes her look like a princess. Her hair has big curls and it's all gathered up and pinned atop her head with a few strands framing her beautiful face. Her veil is trailing down her back it's not covering her face. It seems like she floats down the aisle with her father walking beside her. When they stop short of the place, I stand her father takes her hand and gives it a light kiss. As the priest asks who gives this woman to this man her father speaks up then he lifts her hand from his and lays it in mine. Wow, my wife is beautiful if having babies makes her glow like this, we are going to have a lot of kids.

As we say our vows to each other a light snow starts to fall outside. The reception is in full swing when I pull my wife close to me and we dance our final dance for the night.

"You ready to get out of here and head towards our honeymoon in Hawaii?"

When she gives me a quick kiss and whispers her answer across my skin my slacks tighten. Grabbing her hand, I pull her along behind me making our way to our table so we can tell everyone goodbye.

Our two-week honeymoon flies by and we are soon on a jet headed back to Georgia to start our life together and in a couple of weeks, we'll announce we are going to be welcoming a baby to our family before the end of the year.

CHAPTER EIGHT

April

Married life seems to suit us both well we fall into a normal routine as if we have been married to each other forever. There have been the normal hiccups along the way of who sleeps on what side of the bed. Then one evening when I come home from work the aroma of freshly cooked food isn't the only thing that hits me as I walk in the front door. Somewhere not quite sure where but my wife found a mutt and brought it home with her.

"Ethan it's a small dog it'll be good for the baby they can grow together. Plus, it gives me something else to talk to during the day when Karen is at school or work. Being at home is great but we are way ahead of our friends we are the only married people and we are for sure the only one's having a baby this year."

"First don't try to guilt me into letting you keep the fleabag. You could have done the Spring semester but you chose not to. Sweetheart, a dog is a lot of responsibility especially since we have a baby coming in a few months. I'm not saying yes or no here... But who is going to take care of it when you first have the baby, he or she will demand all our attention?"

"Ethan we can handle a dog he needs to be feed daily and let out to run and do his business. The whole backyard is fenced in so we can just let him out no need to walk him. Think about it is all I'm asking."

Knowing how this is going to play out in the end there's no reason to keep pointing out we don't need a dog. Greta can talk me into just about anything and I do feel sorry for her being stuck at home all day.

It's been a couple of weeks the mutt now has the run of the house and holds my wife's heart completely. Every evening now I brace for impact when opening the front door. Nudging him out of my way I make quick work of dropping all my stuff on the table inside the front door. Today was a baby appointment day and they have become one of my favorite days out of the whole month.

"Ethan you will not believe what I found out today. The nurse told me they can guess the baby's gender off of his or her heart rate."

Watching as she rubs her round little bulge makes me smile "did she happen to tell you what our baby is going to be?"

"She did but do you really want to know who is in here?"

"No, I want to know now. It's only fair as you already know."

"Going off of the heart rate she is convinced it's a boy but the doctor warned me that is not a hundred percent accurate."

Reaching my hand out I touch her stomach "a boy this is great. I'll take him to ball games teach him to play ball."

When she lays her hand over mine, I look at her for the first time really seeing her as the mother to my unborn son.

"For the record Greta, I would have been just as happy if you told me our baby was going to be a girl. We can really start talking about names now which reminds me we need to figure out what the nursery is going to look like my mother keeps asking."

"Well for the record my parents are still not talking to me. At this point Ethan I don't know if they will ever talk to me again but I couldn't lie when they asked if I was pregnant before the wedding."

Watching her pat her belly before she turns to waddle from the room makes me smile but her parents are starting to get on my nerves. They need to be more supportive of their own daughter we did the right thing. Her father and I are sure her mother also knew I was going to ask her to marry me well before we got engaged. It amazes me that people still worry about trivial things when there is a whole new life coming into the world. My parents got over the baby before marriage thing before we walked down the aisle... But we agreed not to tell her parents till after we were married hoping it would help them accept the fact the baby would be coming early per everyone's calculations.

Days turn into weeks and soon it's the start of summer and Greta is becoming very pregnant with each passing day it seems. As May slips by June rolls in with a major heat-wave that no one can escape not even the air system in our home was keeping up with the rising temperatures outside. Those temps outside made my sweet Greta one ill-tempered woman who is almost seven months pregnant. So, like any man who has ever dealt with a hot pregnant wife, I am in search of fans anything to help her make it through the heatwave. My sectary Marlene found me a couple of window fans two towns over from us and I'm going to pick them up after work.

Driving the two hours to the town that has the fan just adds to the not so fun day I've had. The air at work isn't working the temperature isn't dropping any as the sun starts to set. Toss in changing a flat tire on the shoulder of the road and you have a very tired, very hot, very aggravated husband and father to be. Sliding back behind the steering wheel of the car after the young man loads the fans into my trunk I turn home. This damn week can't end fast enough for me once I get a nice whiskey and cigar my weekend will officially begin. Getting back on the interstate traffic is moving at a good speed should get home in time for dinner. Glancing at my watch I notice it's almost time for dinner Greta will looking for me any moment now then my focus is brought back to the present as a station wagon cuts off a tractor-trailer who swerves across the line headed right for me. The last few moments of my life are filled with Greta's smiling face as I was dead on impact.

CHAPTER NINE

Devastation Comes Knocking

It's an hour past when Ethan should be home. Where in the world could that man be, I've stood on my swollen feet for hours cooking dinner and he couldn't even be on time. He knows how hard it is on me with the heat and me being six months pregnant the least he could have done was called to let me know he was running behind. Taking his and my plate back into the kitchen I place in the warmer till he gets home. Settling onto the sofa I prop my feet up and pick the paper up. The doorbell rings clambering to my feet I peek through the curtains to see a state trooper parked out front on the street. Opening the front door, I peer up at the officer

"Hello, Officer, can I help you?"

"Are you Mrs. Ethan Carter?"

"Yes, Sir, is my husband in some kind of trouble?"

"Ma'am, can we talk inside?"

Opening the door, a little more I let the officers in and show them to the living room.

"Here have a seat can I get you, two gentlemen, a drink or something?"

"No ma'am but take a seat we have some news to tell you. Mr. Carter was killed in an accident about an hour ago. We are so sorry for your loss is there anyone we can call for you ma'am?"

The news was nowhere near what I expected from them dropping to my knees I scream for Ethan beg God to give him back to me and our unborn little boy. How can Ethan's life be over when he hasn't even met his son for the first time? We've not had enough time together for one of us to die. This feels like a nightmare and I'm certain it is till my father pulls me into a hug hushing my screams.

"Greta, sweetie, come on get up off the floor your mom has gone to get you something to calm your nerves. Ethan's parents are on their way over there is a lot to be done in the next few days you got to be brave, sweetie. That sounds cruel I know it does but death isn't ever easy no matter how it happens or when it happens."

The silence settles in the room once I sit on the sofa, I keep looking at the paper I had just opened mere minutes ago before my husband was dead. How will our baby ever know how wonderful his father was? Who will teach our little boy to play ball, ride a bike, who will explain girls to him? Ethan can't be gone I have no clue how to live without him my whole life was adjusted when we got married. I went from my parents straight to Ethan's house I've never been alone. Now everyone will expect me to be a single mom, take care of myself and a baby. Being a widow at twenty had never entered my mind no one is a widow at such a young age.

Evening turns into night the house is full of family and friends they all have the best of intentions but right now I would like nothing more than to be alone. When people started to show up, I'd moved into Ethan's chair so no one would sit in it. It has been my favorite sitting place since the first time we came here after a date the chair smells just like Ethan with a hint of cigar and his cologne.

"Greta, I made you a small plate you need to try to eat a little for the baby."

"Thank you, Karen." Taking the plate from her my eyes scan the room Jason isn't here. "Karen, where is Jason? Has someone told him what has happened? Oh, he will not take this well at all they were so close."

"Jason was told Greta he just didn't want to come in earlier said he'd see you tomorrow. You are right though he is very upset never saw him cry before tonight and you know we've been together forever. Is there anything you'd like for me to do for you or get you?"

"Can you make everyone leave? I want to go bed but don't want anyone sitting in his chair."

"Greta, you can ask everyone to leave. It is your home. They are all here trying to take care of you but I understand you'd rather be alone right now. Would you like for me to ask people politely to leave?"

"Would you? Also, could you stay the night here with me? I don't want to be around people but don't want to be in the house alone either."

In less than an hour, Karen had everyone out of the house and I'm lying in our bed with Ethan's pillow pulled close to me. My husband will never lay beside me in our bed in our house he is gone forever. I'd seen him less than twenty-four hours ago when he'd left for work promising to bring home some extra fans to help with the heat. Now he will never walk through the front door again. Reality hits me really quickly where will I live after this; I can't afford this house my parents are barely talking to me tonight was the first time since the wedding. Rubbing my stomach, I talk softly to the baby "don't worry about anything sweetheart mom will take care of all this before you get here." that's the last thought I have before falling to asleep into a cry induced sleep.

Processing your spouse is gone is a lot harder than one would think and as his next of kin, there are so many decisions to be made for the funeral. Ivan stopped by early this morning to let me know he was going to go verify identity for me to spare me of that. We had been advised already it would be best to have a closed casket funeral. There will be no last chance to see his beautiful face never another moment to look into his deep brown eyes. No more whispers from his lips about how much he loves me. Curled up in his chair I watch as people float in and out of the house throughout the day. Very few seek me out but then again what can anyone say that hasn't been repeated to me a hundred times already.

"Greta, sorry I didn't come in last night but no one would have wanted to be around me. Have you eaten anything today? Maybe you'd like to go out for a walk or something. Anything has got to be better than sitting in here with all this going on around you."

When my eyes met Jason's, tears swell in both our eyes. "There's some stuff that they say I have to do but how am I post to know how to buy a casket? In some ways, you knew Ethan more than I did can you help me pick out his clothes and go to the funeral home with me?"

"Sure, we can do that together but you have to promise not to tell anyone if I cry," he says with a sad smile on his face

"Deal if you promise to do the same for me. Give me a few minutes and I'll be ready to leave."

Returning back to my home we sit in the driveway looking towards the front door.

"At least it looks like most of them have left for the day. Greta, you got to make me a promise Ethan would want me to step in here. If you ever need anything call me if it is just to have someone to sit with you through a day or night you can't handle being alone. Ethan was my best friend my whole life some people say that but it's not true but we were truly best friends forever. I'd love to help you with the baby when it's born if you need something tell me, I can't ever be him but I would love to be part of his child's life."

Promising Jason I go into the house closing the world out for the night. Tomorrow I have to be around everyone as we all plan to tell Ethan goodbye forever... But for tonight I'm going to hold his pillow close and pretend he's still here.

Sitting in a chair at the front of the church we were married in four short months ago is an ere feeling. All of our friends and family come by to tell me how sorry they are. It's empty words but there's nothing better for them to say. Way too soon it's time to say our final goodbye to Ethan and it's taking all my willpower not to drop to my knees to beg God one more time to give him back.

Sitting in one of the chairs beside the grave where the casket sets my mother is on one side of me while Karen is on the other side with my father standing behind me with Jason beside him. Standing I take a small handful of dirt and sprinkle it across his casket as I whisper "I'll love you forever, Ethan. You were my one, forever."

CHAPTER TEN

Time Marches On

It's been a month since Ethan passed away and today, we have a meeting with the family lawyer. This day has been marked on the calendar in the kitchen for a week. His parents have been so supportive but he was their son and they will want his stuff as much as I want certain things of his for our baby. Karen had offered to go with me but I'd waved her off people can't keep holding my hand through the rough times in life. This is the life I was given to live so it's best to learn that now before the baby gets here.

Parking the car in the parking area for the office building I get out of the car smooth my dress out then give my back one good stretch before walking towards the front of the building where Ivan is waiting on me.

"Was waiting to see if you'd need any help getting out of the car. When Patricia was this pregnant with Ethan, she couldn't get off the sofa without help she was like you all belly."

"No, lucky me. I can still get up by myself it'd be a little hard if I needed help."

As he holds the door open Patricia comes over and gives me a small hug "you ready for this sweetie? Don't know why our son made this meeting to happen so soon after his passing. Men guess we never figure them out it seems."

Once we are all seated around the table the lawyer lays the file down on the table.

"First I want to offer my condolences on the loss of your husband and your son. He was a wonderful young man and we were friends for many years. Ethan left nothing undone he planned everything in advance when I asked him about it once he said we never know what tomorrow will bring. His passing had made me realize he is right about that for sure. Now let's get down to business."

"First let's go over what he left for his wife. Greta, you now own the home you currently live in along with everything in it. He set up a monthly income for you. It's a sizeable total so it is well more than you will ever need in life per his request my accounting team will be the ones who will issue the monthly payments to your bank account in the sum of one thousand and two hundred dollars a month. If for some reason this amount doesn't cover your expenses for the month please contact the office. You also own the car you currently have in your possession."

"Then he provided for his unborn child if something happened. His portion of the family business off thirty-three percent is for the child or children born. Or in this case to be born."

"That leaves you, Ivan and Patricia, this was a hard one for him to do because he was positive that being his parents was enough reward in itself? Just so we know that wasn't my joke. He left his share in the family vacation home to you both to be done with as you all see fit. That brings us to the end of his will are there any questions about any of his wishes?"

We all look at each other in more shock than they seem to be in. I own a home there will be no worry about how to afford to take care of our son in the future. Ethan truly did plan for everything he had proved that over and over in our relationship but this is way more than I ever expected to walk away with. Having our son would have been more than enough.

When we get to the parking lot Patricia stops beside my car "Greta will you call us when the baby is coming? We'd love to be part of their life it'll be like we still have a small part of Ethan still here with us."

"Mister and Mrs. Carter this baby will need all of us to tell him how wonderful and amazing his dad was. This baby is half your son and I'd never take him away from you all."

"You keep calling the baby a him why?"

"Oh, one of the nurses said the baby would be a boy so I guess it just stuck. When I go into labor, we will call you right away."

———

Soon long summer days start to shift into short cooler days. The baby is due in about three weeks and it's so hard to believe that much time has passed since Ethan passed away. There are days I catch myself watching for him in the evening or sitting in the bed staring at a hole in the bathroom door waiting on him to walk through it. People keep telling me it will get easier with time but that's not true every day my heart still cries for him. Our bed seems so large without him in it I've yet to change the pillowcase on his pillow the scent of him is starting to fade away.

Karen moved in a couple of weeks back to be here when it's time to have this little one. Jason assigned himself the official nursery builder he painted it a light blue put all the furniture together and moved it all a couple of dozen times until I was happy with it. He and Karen even picked up a bassinet for my room so the baby would be close to me at night at first. Seems we've all done everything that needs to be done before the baby arrives.

The nursery has officially been done for two weeks now and I'm standing in the door looking at everything that one little person needs. Standing there rubbing my back I scream out as the first contraction rips through my body as I double over in pain. Karen and Jason both come running. Jason stops short this isn't the part I promised to be part of.

Once I'm settled in labor and delivery Karen calls the Carter's and my parents to let them know where we are. When the nurse informs me, this is the beginning of the labor part I'm certain she is mistaking as this pain has to be the worst any woman has ever had before. With all my begging the nurse had finally let my mom in the room with me but Karen wasn't allowed as she was unwed.

The longest day and night of my life ended after eighteen hours twenty-two minutes with the birth of our little boy Ethan Ivan Carter born September 11 1959 weighing in at eight pounds and five ounces and twenty-one inches long with long dark hair. He looks so much like his dad it made me cry the first time I held him in my arms. When they moved me to my room Ivan stopped by my room before leaving the hospital.

"You doing okay Greta? This isn't ideal for any of us but thank you for that gift. He looks so much like his dad and

I'm honored you gave him my name. Patricia will be by tomorrow sometime she'll more than likely mother you the whole time you're here if she gets to be too much let me know."

"Thank you, Mister Carter, for everything but most of all for Ethan he was the man of my dreams and I'll make sure little Ethan knows all about him."

EPILOGUE

It's Ethan's third birthday and he's chasing Jason around in the backyard that has turned into a small petting zoo thanks to his grandparents both sets.

There's not one day that passes that Ethan doesn't cross my mind he still lives inside my heart I'm certain there will never be another man for me.

Every night I thank God for the gift of Ethan he was the best husband ever and, in the end, he gave me the most amazing gift.

Our son is just like his dad in every way sometimes I look at him and think he could almost be him.

Ethan gave me the best gift ever with little Ethan; a *Love to Last a Lifetime*.

It's a love that will never end.

No matter what.

The End

ACKNOWLEDGMENTS

Peace, Love, and Butterflies
In loving memory of our mom

Printed in Great Britain
by Amazon

17575216R00038